Bubby's Puddle Pond

A Tortuga's Tale of the Desert

Carol Hageman

Illustrated by

Nathaniel P. Jensen

D1305976

Niña Story Books, LLC
carol.hageman@gmail.com
www.NinaStoryBooks.com

Publisher's Cataloging-In-Publication Data
   Names: Hageman, Carol, 1954- | Jensen, Nathaniel P., illustrator.
   Title: Bubby's puddle pond : a tortuga's tale of the desert / Carol Hageman ; illustrated by Nathaniel P. Jensen.
   Description: [Tempe, Arizona] : Niña Story Books, LLC, [2017] | Interest age level: 004-008. | Summary: "In the desert, a tortoise named Bubby learns how to trust his friends and himself."--Provided by publisher.
   Identifiers: ISBN 978-0-9989851-0-7 | ISBN 978-0-9989851-1-4 (ebook)
   Subjects: LCSH: Turtles--Juvenile fiction. | Trust--Juvenile fiction. | Friendship--Juvenile fiction. | Deserts--Juvenile fiction. | CYAC: Turtles--Fiction. | Trust--Fiction. | Friendship--Fiction. | Deserts--Fiction.
   Classification: LCC PZ10.3.H34 Bu 2017 (print) | LCC PZ10.3.H34 (ebook) | DDC [E]--dc23

Printed in the United States of America

Illustrator: Nathaniel P. Jensen
Cover Design & Page Layout: Jeff Yesh
Editor: Conrad J. Storad
Curriculum Guide: Jean Kilker
Proofreaders: Cristy Bertini and RuthAnn Raitter
Project Manager: Patti Crane

Produced by Story Monsters LLC

In memory of

Martín Mares

1963-2013

Acknowledgments

For my mom and dad. Thank you for instilling in me the love of books and birds.

Many thanks to everyone at Story Monsters LLC for making my first book possible.

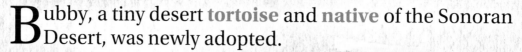

Bubby, a tiny desert **tortoise** and **native** of the Sonoran Desert, was newly adopted.

It was summer. His new owner, Erin, brought him home in a shoe box. She gently lifted him out to see his new **habitat**.

4

"Perfect," he thought.
"Best of all, it has a puddle pond!"

Bubby was hungry and tired from his long journey. He decided to munch on some grass before heading to his **burrow**. In his path was a big garden hose.

I hope I can make it over, he thought.

A little bird landed close.

"Hi, my name is Katie. I'm a **cactus wren**. Who are you? What are you doing?

Can we be friends?" she asked.

"Sure, my name is Bubby."

"Just a little farther, Bubby. You can do it!" Katie yelled.

Plop!

"Hooray! You made it over," shouted Katie. "Now, let's play. We can fly up into the big **mesquite tree**..."

"Wait!" Bubby shouted, "I can't fly."

"Well then, I'll be on my way. See you later," said Katie.

7

Bubby's tummy was full. He headed to his **burrow** for a nap.

Inside was a surprise. A little bunny was shaking, huddled in the corner.

"Hi there, what is your name?" asked Bubby.

"Cotton," whispered the bunny.

"Don't be scared, Cotton. I will share my **burrow** with you. My name is Bubby."

The two little friends shared the **burrow** for a short nap.

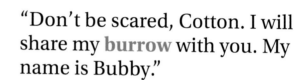

One fall day, Bubby watched as Erin prepared a **hibernation box**. She wanted to give Bubby extra protection to make it through the winter because he was so young.

Bubby was sleepy. He was ready for **hibernation**.

Months later, Bubby pushed open the door. He was greeted by the bright sunshine. Katie and Cotton were waiting. Wasting no time, the trio scurried off to the **burrow**!

Inside was another surprise.

A little **Mediterranean gecko** smiled at the friends.

"Hello, my name is Dottie. I'm making this old house really spiffy."

"But this is my house," Bubby interrupted. "I share it with Katie and Cotton."

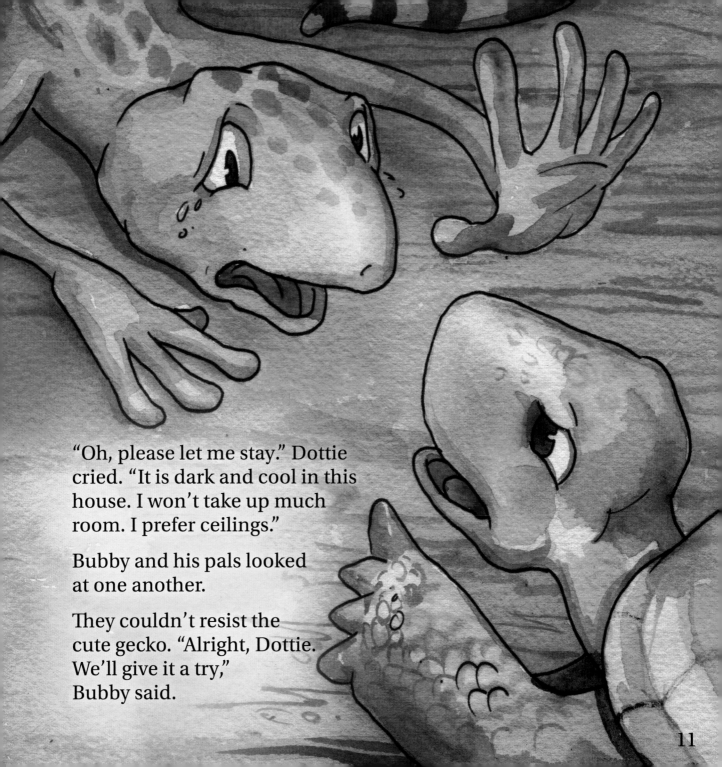

"Oh, please let me stay." Dottie cried. "It is dark and cool in this house. I won't take up much room. I prefer ceilings."

Bubby and his pals looked at one another.

They couldn't resist the cute gecko. "Alright, Dottie. We'll give it a try," Bubby said.

The new friends went outside to play. Suddenly, the clouds grew dark. Thunder rumbled in the distance. Dottie and Cotton ran to the safe, dry **burrow**. Katie flew to the big **mesquite tree**.

Bubby wanted to feel the rain for the first time. He loved getting a shower bath.

His first drink of fresh rain water tasted so good.

The little pals met after the storm.

They saw a tiny quail perched in the big mesquite tree.

"Hello there, my name is Bubby. These are my friends Dottie, Katie, and Cotton. What's your name?"

14

"My name is Bernie," said the tiny **Gambel's quail**.

Katie was excited to see another bird. "Baby Bernie quail, come play with us!"

Bernie flew down to the puddle pond. The splashing began. From then on, the friends met daily to explore and play.

Summer quickly turned to fall. Erin prepared Bubby's special box once again.

Bubby knew it was time. He looked at the **burrow** and wondered if someday he would **hibernate** there.

But, turning toward the box, he saw the soft hay and leaves and crawled in. Once inside, he fell fast asleep.

15

A few months passed. Bubby began to stir.

He was eager to see his friends. When he pushed the door open, he was greeted with two big eyes instead!

Bubby was scared!

"Mr. Tortuga, come out of your shell. I want to play ball with you," said the little Boston Terrier.

She placed a ball in front of his nose. Bubby slowly gave it a bump. It rolled.

"Do it again!" said the pup excitedly.

"Bebe, come!" Erin called from the door.

"We'll play later," the dog said to Bubby.

Running toward the house, she turned and asked, "What is your name Mr. Tortuga?"

"Bubby!" he answered.

Finally, Bubby found his friends. He told them about meeting Bebe. They thought he was very brave.

17

Rainy days in summer are welcomed in the desert. The air is cooler.

One such day, the pals were playing in the puddle pond. Suddenly, the gate opened with a loud creeeek.

A man wearing a large hat walked into the yard. His arms were full of equipment.

The friends froze for a split second, then hurried to the **burrow**.

"Where is Bebe?" Bubby wondered. "She could bark at the man and scare him away."

"What should we do?" the friends said in one voice.

A decision had to be made.

They all agreed that Bubby should investigate. After all, he had a shell to protect himself.

19

Bubby carefully crept closer, remaining out of sight. He heard the man talking to the tree.

"You tell me what branches to remove. It will make you feel lighter," the man said in a kind voice.

The man trimmed the tree. Then he carried a big armload of branches toward the gate. Bubby followed from a safe distance.

Bubby had always wondered what was on the other side of the gate. He explored everywhere. He couldn't wait to tell his friends about his big adventure.

On his way back, Bubby took a break under a bush. Soon he was fast asleep.

When he woke, the sun was setting low in the sky. Bubby ran to the gate.

It was closed!

Meanwhile, Bubby's friends were still hiding. All was quiet. They came out of the **burrow** for a look.

"Wow," Katie said. "The big **mesquite tree** looks happy!" All agreed.

Then, off to the puddle pond they went.

"Bubby! Bubby!!" the friends shouted. They searched everywhere.

They could not find him. "Don't give up," said Dottie. "I'll ask my gecko friends for help. We'll search all night."

Dottie returned at sunrise. The news was the same. No Bubby.

Cotton and Katie wondered if he might be sleeping under the last pile of branches.

"Let's look."

Just then, they heard Bebe barking. Erin and her mom were walking next to the man in the big hat. He was carrying Bubby.

"Martín, thank you so much for finding Bubby!" said Erin.

"Luckily, I spotted him in the front yard when I returned," Martín replied.

Bubby was back! The puddle pond pals were together again.

That summer was extra busy. Bubby added a new room in the **burrow**.

A third cycle of **hibernation** was beginning.

Erin held Bubby close. "Bubby you are a big boy now. I think the time has come for you to **hibernate** in your **burrow**."

"Bye, little fellow," she whispered. "See you in the spring."

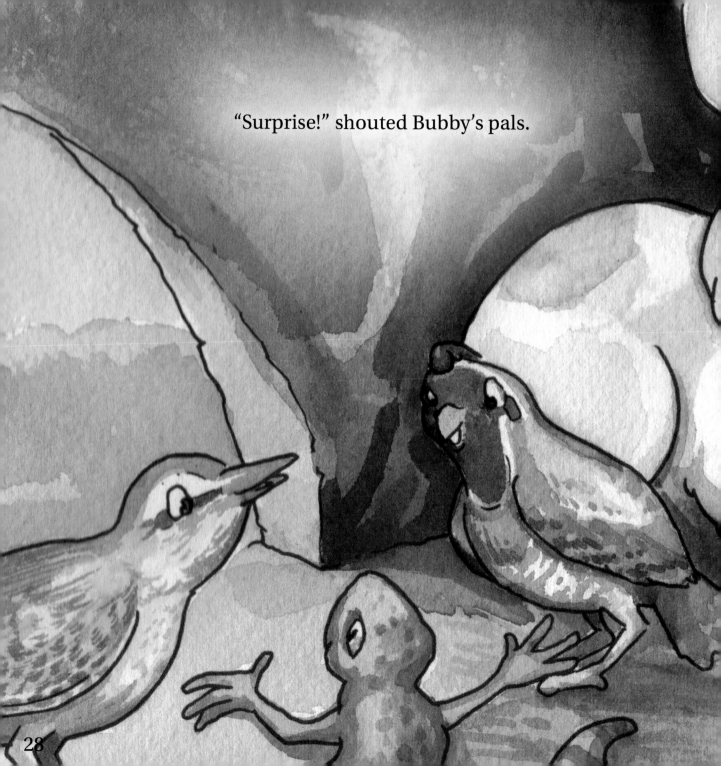

"Surprise!" shouted Bubby's pals.

His friends were waiting for him in the burrow. They never got to go with Bubby when he hibernated in his box. There was never enough room for everyone. Now, there was plenty of room for all the puddle pond pals.

Bubby was ready for a winter of sweet dreams.

Learn More About the Desert Tortoise

Two types of desert tortoises live in Arizona. The Sonoran desert tortoise (Gopherus morafkai) lives in the southern and western parts of the state. It also lives in parts of northern Mexico. The Mojave desert tortoise (Gopherus agassizii) lives in a small part of northwestern Arizona. It also lives in parts of Nevada, Utah, and California.

Desert tortoises are herbivores. They eat plants. It is important to provide a pet desert tortoise with a variety of appropriate foods—the same as what a tortoise would eat in the wild. Grass is an important part of a healthy diet for a desert tortoise. They need other foods, too. For a complete list of appropriate foods, go to the Arizona Game and Fish Department website at www.azgfd.com. The site also provides an entire section on how to properly care for a captive desert tortoise.

Desert tortoises enjoy a good soak now and then, but not so much that they have difficulty keeping their heads above water. The dish should be large enough for the tortoise to sit in. Never let your desert tortoise get near a swimming pool or ornamental pond. They cannot swim. A desert tortoise can drown in deep water.

Domestic pets and wild animals can be a danger to all tortoises. Keep a watchful eye on your pet. It's especially important to keep dogs away from your desert tortoise if they show aggressive tendencies, no matter if your tortoise is small or large. Dogs can quickly injure or kill a desert tortoise.

Wild desert tortoises often dig burrows to create shelters from the searing desert heat and frigid winter temperatures. A pet desert tortoise needs a shelter for the same protection. The shelter should not be too big. Tortoises like snug, cozy homes. The entrance should be elevated above the surrounding ground. You don't want rainwater to flood the shelter.

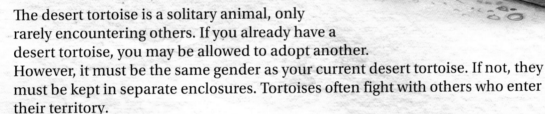

The desert tortoise is a solitary animal, only rarely encountering others. If you already have a desert tortoise, you may be allowed to adopt another. However, it must be the same gender as your current desert tortoise. If not, they must be kept in separate enclosures. Tortoises often fight with others who enter their territory.

As with any pet, always wash your hands after handling a tortoise.

Adoption Information

You must be a permanent resident of Arizona to adopt a desert tortoise. The creatures are non-traditional pets. They are fascinating animals to observe. Families can gain a new appreciation of desert wildlife by caring for a Sonoran desert tortoise and watching its natural behaviors.

Tortoises can live for many years. Some in captivity live longer than humans. For that reason, before adopting a desert tortoise, you must do your research. Study and learn as much as possible about desert tortoise care.

Desert tortoises are typically available for adoption from April 1 to September 30. They hibernate during colder months. That leaves you plenty of time during the winter months to create a habitat for your new pet.

Desert tortoises cannot be removed from Arizona. If you are a desert tortoise custodian and are moving from Arizona, you must return the desert tortoise to one of the adoption facilities or find a new home with another qualified family.

Releasing a captive desert tortoise into the wild is illegal. Doing so endangers wild tortoises. Pet tortoises can spread diseases and parasites and disrupt uniquely adapted genetics in wild populations.

There are many desert tortoises in captivity. Hundreds of them need homes. Visit www.azgfd.gov/tortoise for detailed information about the adoption process.

Desert tortoise adoption facilities:

Phoenix, Kingman, Bullhead City, Lake Havasu, and Yuma:
Toll-free: 844-896-5730; TAP@azgfd.gov

Prescott: Heritage Park Zoological Sanctuary 928-778-4242

Tucson: Arizona-Sonora Desert Museum 520-883-3062; www.desertmuseum.org/programs/tap.html

Glossary of Words

Burrow – A hole or tunnel in the ground. The home for a desert tortoise.

Cactus wren – A species of wren that is native to the southwestern United States.

Gambel's quail – A species of quail that is native to the southwestern United States.

Habitat – The natural home or environment of an animal.

Hibernate – To spend the winter in close quarters in a dormant condition.

Hibernation box – A small container for a hatchling or young tortoise to hibernate in during the winter.

Mediterranean gecko – A small spotted, nocturnal, gecko that eats insects. It has large eyes and sticky toe pads to help it climb on vertical walls and ceilings.

Mesquite tree – A common tree of the desert southwest.

Native – A species found only within a particular region.

Tortoise – The name scientists give to turtles that live on dry land.

Tortuga – The Spanish word for tortoise.

Curriculum Guide

Reading

Read Bubby's story several times. The first time you go through the story, use the pictures to tell the story and make predictions about what you think is happening as you turn the pages. The second time, concentrate on the highlighted words and discuss their meaning, so the vocabulary knowledge creates a smooth reading session. For example, what is hibernation? Use the glossary. The third time, read the whole story.

Writing

Let's spell the word, desert. **D-e-s-e-r-t.** How do you know the difference between desert and dessert? An easy way to remember is that there is an extra "s" in the word "dessert," because the best desserts have both sugar and spice, but a desert only has sand!

Bubby and his friends have many good characteristics. Discuss or write about instances of generosity, friendliness, and bravery. How have you seen each of these characteristics personally?

Research

Where is the Sonoran Desert?
Can you find it on a map?

The internet is a terrific tool to use to find information about anything you want to know! Let's see what we can learn about desert tortoises by visiting:

National Geographic Kids:
kids.nationalgeographic.com/animals/

Arizona-Sonora Desert Museum:
www.desertmuseum.org/kids/oz/long-fact-sheets/Desert%20Tortoise.php

Write three new things you discovered about desert tortoises from researching these websites.

Hands On

Tortoise Bookmark: Create a tortoise bookmark with scrap felt or paper. You need tan, brown, and dark green.

1. Cut a piece of tan-colored felt that is 3 inches by 5 inches long.

2. Cut a 1-inch diameter green circle.

3. Cut five circles from brown, each ½-inch in diameter.

4. Cut one tail piece from brown, about ½-inch long.

5. Draw circle markings on the larger green circle to make a tortoise.

6. Draw eyes on one ½-inch circle and claws on the other four smaller circles.

7. Slightly overlap and then glue the small pieces under the larger green circle to create a tortoise shape.

8. Glue the tortoise to one end of the tan strip.

Use your bookmark to keep track of your place while reading Bubby's Puddle Pond.

More activities available on www.NinaStoryBooks.com

About the Author

Inspired by her lifelong love of wildlife and the outdoors, first-time author **Carol Hageman** has written a book that's enjoyable for children up to and including second grade. When she decided to write the story of a tortoise in *Bubby's Puddle Pond: A Tortuga's Tale of the Desert*, she drew on some of the real-life behaviors she witnessed. Carol wanted to pass along her curiosity and enthusiasm to today's young readers—many of whom may have never seen an animal in the wild. She realizes how special it was being raised on a farm. It gave her appreciation and love of nature that she hopes other children can experience.

Carol is a floral designer and once owned a florist shop. She has experience in the landscape industry and is a master gardener. She and her husband, Bernie, currently live in Tempe, Arizona. Their daughter, Erin, and her husband, Erich, live in Phoenix, Arizona. In her free time, Hageman practices yoga, rides horses, and loves to read. www.NinaStoryBooks.com

About the Illustrator

Nathaniel P. Jensen is an illustrator, designer, animator, muralist, and fine art oil painter. Having freelanced for 25 years, he has painted murals on buildings as high as 60-feet tall, animated for feature films, and illustrated for newspapers and magazines nationwide. He enjoys playing around with children's book ideas and has created illustrations for more than 20 children's titles. Learn more at www.natepjensen.com.

About the Editor

Conrad J. Storad is an award-winning author and editor of more than 50 science and nature books for children and young adults, including *Monster in the Rocks*; *Gator, Gator, Second Grader (Classroom Pet...or Not?)*; the "USA Best Book," *Rattlesnake Rules*; and the ONEBOOKAZ for Kids 2012 selection, *Arizona Way Out West & Witty*. He holds an undergraduate degree in mass media communication from the University of Akron and a master's degree in mass communication/science journalism from Arizona State University's Walter Cronkite School of Journalism. He resides in Ohio with his wife, Laurie, and their rescue wiener dog, Frankie. Learn more at www.conradstorad.com.